9/12

SEED
by
SEED

The Legend and Legacy of
John "Appleseed" Chapman

By Esmé Raji Codell

Illustrations by Lynne Rae Perkins

Greenwillow Books, *An Imprint of* HarperCollins*Publishers*

To Johnny A.—*E. R. C.*

For friends and neighbors whose love and persistence
bring forth so many kinds of fruit—*L. R. P.*

Selected Resources and Acknowledgments

Chapman, Frank O. "John Chapman (Johnny Appleseed)." Talk presented at the Brooke County West Virginia
Historical Association, 20 April 1967. http://wcbd.hypermart.net/applecrest/johnny1.html

Greenwood, Barbara, and Heather Collins. *A Pioneer Sampler: The Daily Life of a Pioneer Family in 1840.*
New York: Houghton Mifflin, 1994.

Haley, W. D. "Johnny Appleseed: A Pioneer Hero." *Harper's New Monthly Magazine,* November 1871, vol. 0043,
issue 258 (pp. 830–836). http://mason.gmu.edu/~drwillia/apple/ja5sm.html

Lawlor, Laurie, and Mary Thompson. *The Real Johnny Appleseed.* Morton Grove, IL: Albert Whitman & Company, 1995.

Means, Howard. *Johnny Appleseed: The Man, the Myth, the American Story.* New York: Simon & Schuster, 2011.

Peck, Catherine, ed. *QPB Treasury of North American Folktales.* Rantoul, IL: Quality Paperback Book Club, 1998.

Pollan, Michael. *The Botany of Desire: A Plant's-Eye View of the World.* New York: Random House, 2002.

Price, Robert. *Johnny Appleseed: Man & Myth.* Urbana, OH: Urbana University Press, 2001. First published 1954
by Peter Smith Publisher, Inc.

Tunis, Edwin. *Frontier Living: An Illustrated Guide to Pioneer Life in America, including Log Cabins, Furniture,
Tools, Clothing, and More.* Guilford, CT: The Lyons Press, 2000. First published 1961 by Thomas Y. Crowell.

Special thanks to the Johnny Appleseed Society and the Johnny Appleseed Educational Center & Museum,
both at Urbana University in Ohio, for their resources and support. And thanks to Ren Brabanec, who dressed up
like Johnny Appleseed, walked back and forth, and pretended to plant a tree.

Seed by Seed: The Legend and Legacy of John "Appleseed" Chapman. Text copyright © 2012 by Esmé Raji Codell.
Illustrations copyright © 2012 by Lynne Rae Perkins. All rights reserved. Manufactured in China. For information address
HarperCollins Children's Books, a division of HarperCollins Publishers, 10 East 53rd Street, New York, NY 10022.
www.harpercollinschildrens.com
Watercolor and gouache were used to create the full-color art. Additional media included embroidery, woodcarvings, burlap, and secondhand book pages.
The text type is New Aster.
Library of Congress Cataloging-in-Publication Data: Codell, Esmé Raji, (date). Seed by seed: the legend and legacy of
John "Appleseed" Chapman / by Esmé Raji Codell ; illustrations by Lynne Rae Perkins. p. cm. "Greenwillow Books."
ISBN 978-0-06-145515-5 (trade ed.)—ISBN 978-0-06-145516-2 (lib. ed.) [1. Appleseed, Johnny, 1774–1845—Juvenile literature.
2. Apple growers—United States—Biography—Juvenile literature. 3. Frontier and pioneer life—Middle West—Juvenile literature.]
I. Perkins, Lynne Rae, ill. II. Title. SB63.C46C63 2012   634.11'092—dc23 [B] 2011033653

12 13 14 15 16 SCP 10 9 8 7 6 5 4 3 2 1 First Edition   Greenwillow Books

*Anyone can count the seeds in an apple,
but no one knows how many apples are in a seed.*

WHEN we look out of our windows,
what do we see?

Tall buildings, stores, and parking lots.

Buses and cars speeding by.

Red lights and green lights and yellow lights and white lights.

Our country is hard and electrical and moving.

But it was not always this way.

Once it was a tangle,

a tangle,

a tangle,

of roots and branches and wide tree trunks.

Once, you could not hear the engines of airplanes in the sky,
or the sounds of phones ringing.
Maybe you could catch the creaking of a wagon wheel,
straining against the ruts in the road,
or the fall of an axe against wood.

The bark of a dog.

The crackle of a campfire.

The chattering of squirrels, the pecking of a sapsucker,

the slapping of water against a riverbank.

Or the sound of the play of leaves, turning silver-gray green in the breeze,

a *sh-hh-hhh* like whispered secrets for the bees to carry off.

The moon shone on the snow
until the land glowed like a pearl.
The stars glinted in the sky,
and the candles flickered
from their lamps.

And in this quiet, tree-bough-tangled world,
the world before the cement was poured
and the lights turned on,
there lived a man of his time:
John Chapman, better known
as Johnny Appleseed.

THE tales of Johnny Appleseed are three parts legend,
one part fact, stories we're not *sure* are true.
But the man, John Chapman, was real.
He was born on September 26, 1774, in Massachusetts.

He never drove a car
or sent a basketball flying through a hoop.
He never acted in front of a camera.
He never wore a medal.
He grew apples, and offered them to the pioneers heading west.

But wait. So what?
A farmer. Why should we remember him
today, more than two hundred years later,
and call him a hero?

I will whisper
the answer to you,
a secret silver-gray green:
He lived by example.

And of the many footsteps he took across
the frontier in his bare and knobby feet,
he left five for us to fill:

USE WHAT
YOU HAVE.

SHARE WHAT
YOU HAVE.

RESPECT NATURE.

TRY TO MAKE PEACE
WHERE THERE IS WAR.

YOU CAN REACH YOUR DESTINATION
BY TAKING SMALL STEPS.

No one is certain why he began his work of planting apple trees. He claimed that spirits and angels told him to be a messenger of peace and to grace the way to the west with an offering of fruit.

What we do know is that by doing the same small act of planting seeds every day, Johnny Appleseed changed the landscape of our nation. Seed by seed, deed by deed.

WHAT examples did he plant for us?

USE WHAT YOU HAVE

·∴·

Most apples around the start of the nineteenth century were grown for making cider. John Chapman started his nurseries of apple trees by obtaining apple seeds from owners of cider presses in western Pennsylvania, who were just going to throw the seeds away.

Chapman dressed in coffee and potato sacks or wore used clothing that was given to him by people trading for his trees. Some say he carried his tin cooking pot on his head like a hat. He had a style all his own.

CHAPMAN was rich in coin, and rich in friends. He sold and traded trees to pioneers, but if a person could not afford them, Chapman would still allow that person to take saplings and pay when and if he or she was able. Chapman had eleven brothers and sisters, and they helped one another out when they could.

Besides his love of apples, Chapman also had a strong affection for reading, especially books by a religious man named Emanuel Swedenborg, who preached love, tolerance, and faith.

It is said that John Chapman used his open shirt as a pouch to carry his books. It is also said that he ripped books into chapters in order to circulate them between settlers. He liked to gather children and their families around him and delight them with a story time, "news right fresh from heaven." In this way, he was the frontier's first librarian!

JOHN CHAPMAN lived most of his life outdoors. He was a vegetarian and also had a vast knowledge of herbs and their uses. Besides planting apples, John Chapman liked to plant fennel, a bulb that smells strongly of licorice and that he believed had medicinal powers. In some parts of the country, this fast-spreading plant is still called "Johnny weed."

Dog Fennel
ALSO CALLED
"Johnny weed"

Pennyroyal

Mullein

It is said that he lived in peace with the animals. Legend has it that he released a wolf from a trap, and for a long time afterward the wolf tamely followed him wherever he went.

Once he slept at one end of a log with a bear and her cub at the other.

Another time, when he noticed that his campfire was singeing the wings of mosquitoes, he doused the flames in order to save the insects.

When he saw that an animal was being abused, he
would buy that animal, nurse it back to health, and
find it a good home. The only animal he was known
to have killed was a rattlesnake. Though he acted in
self-defense, he was said to have always felt badly
for having taken that life.

The Native Americans respected him for his
spiritual bond with his surroundings, his kinship
with all that grew and lived.

J OHN CHAPMAN moved freely between Native American
and pioneer communities, and he was trusted by both.

He warned each side of the other's impending attack, usually by walking through a room and reciting a mysterious rhyme.

JOHN CHAPMAN journeyed hundreds of miles across state lines on his own two feet, or by canoe on the waterways, planting and maintaining his tree nurseries over a hundred thousand square miles. His trees flowered and fruited across the Ohio River Valley, and they were shared and carried off to homesteads far and wide.

You can reach your destination

... by taking small steps

He grew so many apple trees that chances are any apple you eat today is from a descendant of a tree planted by Johnny Appleseed.

After catching pneumonia during an especially cold winter in 1845, John Chapman passed away. His sweet spirit lives on in the apples we eat and in the seeds we plant to make our country and our world a better place.

SEED by seed, deed by deed,
Johnny Appleseed changed the landscape of a nation.
And now it's your turn.
One small deed, every day.

What seed will you plant?

A Johnny Appleseed Anniversary

SEPTEMBER 26TH, the day
of John Chapman's birth, is a day to celebrate!
Start by making a Johnny Appleseed pledge. Similar
to a New Year's resolution, this is a promise to do one small deed
every day that can change our country for the better. Write it out on some
pretty parchment paper, butcher block paper, or a brown paper bag. Decorate
with apple stamps (just cut apples in half, and dip the flat side in red, green, or yellow
tempera paint). Or cut out a circle of white paper to fit inside a red paper plate. Write your
pledge on the white paper and glue it inside the red plate. Punch a hole in the top of the red
plate and, through the hole, string a couple of green construction paper leaves on a brown pipe
cleaner so it looks like an apple. Hang and display your pledge all year round!

Of course, no Appleseed anniversary would be complete without something apple-y to eat: maybe apple
butter on toast, or applesauce. But Johnny's favorite, apple pie, is easy enough to make. Slice or cube
8–10 peeled apples of your favorite variety and put them in a big bowl. Add a ½ cup brown sugar and a
½ cup white sugar to the bowl, and mix well with your friendliest spoon. Add some cinnamon or nutmeg,
if you like them. Pour the apple mixture into a frozen pie shell, unless someone has taught you how to
make a homemade piecrust. (You may want to bake the shell for ten minutes before filling, so it doesn't
get soggy.) Cut a stick of hard, cold unsalted butter into little squares, and coat the squares in white flour,
then sprinkle the butter and any extra flour over the top of the apple mixture in the pie shell. Put another
piecrust on top, with a few holes poked for juice and air, or leave the pie open-faced. Put your filled
pie pan on a cookie sheet to catch any drips, and tuck it into a 350-degree oven (ask a grown-up
for help) for a half hour, or until the crust turns brown, or until the kitchen smells like
Johnny Appleseed's idea of heaven. Serve with vanilla ice cream and apple juice or cider
to wash it down. Invite all your friends over to share, and sing the Johnny Appleseed song,
based on a traditional Swedenborgian hymn (you can replace "Lord" with "World"
or "Earth," to taste).

Oh, the Lord is good to me,
And so I thank the Lord
For giving me the things I need:
The sun and the rain and the apple seed.
The Lord is good to me! *Amen*!